THE
SECRET'S OF LIFE

THE SECRET'S OF LIFE

JASMINE BURDINE

ReadersMagnet, LLC

The Secret's of Life
Copyright © 2022 by Jasmine Burdine. All rights reserved.

Published in the United States of America
ISBN Paperback: 978-1-955603-28-7
ISBN eBook: 978-1-955603-27-0

All rights reserved. No part of this publication may be reproduced, stored in a retrieval system or transmitted in any way by any means, electronic, mechanical, photocopy, recording or otherwise without the prior permission of the author except as provided by USA copyright law.

The opinions expressed by the author are not necessarily those of ReadersMagnet, LLC.

ReadersMagnet, LLC
10620 Treena Street, Suite 230 | San Diego, California, 92131 USA
1.619.354.2643 | www.readersmagnet.com

Book design copyright © 2022 by ReadersMagnet, LLC. All rights reserved.
Cover design by Ericka Obando
Interior design by Renalie Malinao

TABLE OF CONTENTS

CHAPTER 1   SORROWS...1
- Ruff Neck 3
- Sorry 5
- Living In Pain 7
- The Lost Boy... 10
- Thirteen 12
- He Stops 14
- Got Lost On The Way 16
- I'm Standing 18
- I Can't Be A Burden 20
- She Walks Alone 22
- He's In The Gang 23
- Don't Tell 24
- Life Keep Passing By 25
- She Scared 26
- Young Kings 28
- Struggle 30
- Crazy Life 32

CHAPTER 2   LOVE GAIN & LOVE LOST 35
- So Many Times 37
- He Gives 39
- Don't Take 41
- Not Herself 43
- Tell Me 45

When I Find Him 47
Bad Habits 49
I Loved You 51
Do You Get Me 54
Brand New 56
Past History 57
From The Distance 59
I'm Past The Point 61
Do You 63
Your Choice 65
He Got You 67
Double Standers 70
Love 71
My Worth 72
My Joy 74
Relationship Not Lasting 75
Don't Stop Believing 76
How Hard 78
Genuine 81

CHAPTER 3   TRAP 83

Alone 85
Keep Your Head Up 86
None The Less 88
The Game 90
I Want Out 91
Life 93
Tell Why Pain Living 95
I See A Different 96
Already Born With A Disadvantage 97
My Father 99
Old Soul 100
God Cry 102
Black Men 103

Broken Queens 104
I Hope 106
I See 107
To The Man Who Made it 108
How Making It Out Started 110
No Negativity 111
I'm Not Suppose Too 112
Sister 114

CHAPTER 1

Sorrows

RUFF NECK

She's ruff neck

Even though she's gorgeous

She's very defiant in everything she does

Intellectual she stays compelling

Oh how marvelous she can be

Given the opportunities that's presented from every door

Even though she had a hard life no doubt

She always stayed composed

Like she was implanting an operation

Like she was playing a game of chess with no remorse

Her mindset was her freedom and her words are her armor

She held herself up so high that no man could touch her

It's not like she didn't want them to

It's the fact she didn't know how to

In all actuality she really had problems

Just going by what her stepdad did to her

Sexually assaulting her verbally abusing her

Even though that's not what screwed up her conscience

It's the fact that her mom knew about it and try to deny it

With all the drama and the domestic violence

Baby girl stayed silent

She was a fighter

Whether they knew it or not

She was going to be a survivor

So, she kept her head up high

And with God's help she was able to reach the sky

Still until this day people would never know

Why she came off harsh or why she stayed to herself

Why she barley said any words like nothing matter to her

It's just they didn't know

She was living a living hell

They didn't know her story

Because she never tells

SORRY

Sorry if I wasn't the best dad, the best dad I could've been

That I couldn't really support you and your mom the way I really wanted too

I was still young trying to figure out who I really am

Since I was drinking a hell of a lot and not really giving a damn

I was like, "fuck being a dad"

I really don't .know how to raise a boy into a man

But for you I'll try

For you I'd give more than I ever can

Because my dad wasn't shit

I didn't care if he lives or die

That man wasn't ever there in my life

But for you I wanted something better

Even if I didn't know how to be

See, you was my king

Every time I hold you

I can feel myself getting all wrapped up inside

Like I was proud to be a dad but mad at the same time

When I look at you

I question why I ever hated you

Why I ever wished you weren't born

It wasn't your fault

Your mom chose not to get that abortion

Now I'm glad she didn't

Now I feel like I could make a difference

Starting with me and you I can change this cycle of a dead-beat dad and I thank you for that

LIVING IN PAIN

She has no name; She covers her pain

with fake laughter and joy

She tries to deny the fact she ever had dreams

That she ever once believed that there's possibilities of her finding real joy

In her own little messed up world

She can't seem to forget the scars

That was marked upon her as a young child

Trying to hide them from her mom so she wouldn't get locked in the basement most of the time

She'll chain her up as if she was a dog

So, she couldn't run away even if she wanted too

Had her begging just to go back to her room

Just to play with her little piece of crap dolls

Just so she could only pretend she was once just a normal little girl again

Her mother always felt like she was a burden on her physically and mentally

So, she never really had love for her

The fact she ends up looking like her dad made her hate her own daughter

That was the only reason why she had her in the first place

But he left her after a few days she was born for a whole another woman

The fact that her daughter was such a beautiful little girl made her upset most of the time only because she looks way better than her mom

So, she stayed doing her best to leave her alone in the house

With different kind of men, she'll sleep with now and then

Some was kind; I'll admit

Then some was worse than her mom

The one's she remembers the most are those who did late night visits to her room

Pretending to read her a bedtime story so her mom wouldn't know

How many times she had cried she lost count

Just as she did when it came to how many men of her mom had given her those special late-night visit

But nobody knows of this little girl

Who hid from her mom so she wouldn't get abused most of the time

Who cried herself to sleep most nights

Who ran away from home through her mind

Because that was a place where she could escape the harsh reality, she was living

If you saw her today

She'll come off as sweet and kind

Loud and outspoken only when it comes to her mind

But yet she'll appear quite like she's not really here

Like she's fighting herself to come back to reality

Yet she's stuck in a trance where she can't be found

Where nobody knows who she is

Therefore she doesn't exist

Only as a lost little girl and that's it

THE LOST BOY

He looked so innocent doing this shit

That no one would believe he was doing this

Taking niggas lives like he was snatchin' up toys at a toy store

He was just a boy only eleven years old

But he looks up to the wrong men

Who took good care of him

They washed him, they clothed him

Teaching him their way on how to be a man

Turning him into a natural born killer

They finally got inside of his head

Now he's like a deadly bomb

It never takes him that much to make him go off with no stop signs

People say you can even hear the ticking of death on his clock ticking

When he walks by or even when he's gunning for you

If you're his target believe me you won't see him

He hides in the dark with a mask over his face with gloves on

Nothing but black on

Ready to hunt like a lion does when it's hungry

He stayed strap no matter who he trusts

When you're dying, he likes to take off his mask to show you who he really is

They'll be like damn you're a little boy

He would be like not no more

Then he'll let another round go off killing them fast

Before they start choking on their own blood

He was the best hit man since no one knew who he was

But once they find out

You could already guess what happen

Yeah, he was eleven years old and as the story was once told

Don't move too fast because you will get caught up just like this little boy once did

THIRTEEN

Thirteen looking like she's in her early twenties

Momma isn't there; she's always out working

Daddy was never there; she never met him in person

Nobody sees what's actually happening

She's thirteen messing around with grow men

Lying about her age so they aren't questioning

She loves feeling wanted

She also loves the attention

She loves the things she gets

That's why she isn't stopping

Her friend is with it

That's where she learns it

Her friend shows her how to really do it

She's thirteen not making no good decisions

She's thirteen and I bet you won't be able to see it

Her body is nicely shaped so every guy wants a piece of it

Got thick hips and thighs so someone is always checking her

Her breast and butt got guys doing a double-take

No matter what sexy tight clothes she wears to bring out her figure

No matter how much makeup she puts on

I can still see the little girl that's hidden

That she's fighting not to be

She's thirteen looking for love in all the wrong ways

She's thirteen and her mom needs to come gets her

So, none of these grown men doesn't snatch her

I can't tell you how many of these girls go missing

I can't tell you how many of these girls end up in prostitution

Running into the wrong guy now there's no solution

I can't tell you how many got so caught up that now they're no longer living

Be careful not everybody is your friend

Be careful thirteen you should start being a kid again

HE STOPS

He stops coming around for me

Now he's actin' like he doesn't even know me

He just stares at me without saying one word to me

He doesn't even smile for me

I can't even make him laugh he just look sad

He was my best friend until his brother pass

Now he's not even here; his mind stays elsewhere

No matter how much I try he just won't open up to me

In his eyes everything is dark and cold with mold

He really thinks he's alone

He thinks no one can feel his pain or understand his reason

He stops showing up to class

He used to come late but he always came

Now he doesn't even bother to come

It's like he doesn't even care anymore

It's like no one can comfort him

It's like he wants to be left alone & depressed

He's starting to believe God was never there for him

If his brother was still here; I know he would be feeling differently

Since he been praying for so long

His brother still got taken away

He lost faith in everything

Everything is a joke, a game

He's playing along not questioning one word anymore

It really hurts seeing him every time when he walks by

It's like seeing a ghost there's no emotions

You could tell his soul is broken

He doesn't even know after the rain storm

There's always a sunny day that comes right after

He's slowly going away

When he goes to his brother grave

He automatically breaks down

He let's all his feelings out

Saying why you had to go and leave me all alone

You know I can't do nothing right when your gone

I miss you while his eyes are full of tears

Even though I can see him

Some how I don't say a word

Instead I just walk right up towards him just set right beside him

He just lay his head on my chest without saying a word

GOT LOST ON THE WAY

Trying to catch the fame she got caught up in the game

Now everybody knows her name she's the night time star

On the corner everyday can't nobody tell her it's a better way

She loves using her body instead of her brain

The money got her in

Got her started got her thinking got her changing her ways

It never used to be this way

She was a smart pretty girl

Always thinking of a brighter world

Until she met a guy who change her whole mind one day

Now there's no turning away

She walks the streets trying to bring him his dreams

He makes her seems she's in control of everything

The money the power the fame gave it in the palm of her hand

  So young so young can't you see it's just a kid living a false dream

No way out no way out that's what other people sees

But to her it's the best place to be

She feels that's her best friend her man her protector

In reality he just another man who is using her abusing her dragging her to her grave

But she can't seem to understand this concept no it won't get through her head

No, she wants to be blind by the wolf in lamb clothing that's how she ends up dead

I'M STANDING

I'm standing up on this stage

To say what's on my mind

I been getting rape and abused

By my mom boyfriend

That she still lives with until this very day

You rape me and took my love away

Made it hard for me to trust a guy that loved me

You said I wouldn't make it

You said I wouldn't be nothing in life but shit in it

But yet here I stand in front of you today

As a senior graduate from college

Yeah, my last year was today

I just wanted to say

Even though you took my virginity away

Put myself self-esteem down

I still made it and I forgive you

But not for you

But for me to set myself free

From not being scared to trust or to love any other man

After what you did to me

I'm free from any pain you gave me

I CAN'T BE A BURDEN

I don't want to go home

Don't want to be a burden

Don't got nothing to tribute

So, what's the point of even going

I'm looking for a way out

Tell me if you see one

Living in a struggle got me fighting just to be someone

But if God can hear my cries at night

Than one day he'll answer my prayers

And life itself can be more alright

Tell me if you can feel my plight

But I'm on a fast lane

I know I'm at risk at losing my life

But if I can put food on my table why not

I do what I got to do

So how can you judge me

If you never walk in my shoes before

Me making seven dollars and fifty cents an hour isn't enough

When the cost of living is constantly going up

I know I put myself in harm way

But I didn't care

If it enables me to give my family a better life

So, I'm stacking up

Rather you see it or not I'm going to make a way

It might not be the best one

But if this is all I know

This is all I been shown

Than where can I go

Tell me do you see a way

Please let me know

Because my clock is ticking

SHE WALKS ALONE

She walks alone

She never really had a home

She by herself in the world that's all she knowns

Her mother died when she was ten

After that it all went down hill from than

She had to become a woman at the age of ten

She got put in foster care each home she went to she ran away from

Only because she was getting sexually abuse

How she felt like nobody understood her life or the pain she was going through

Now she's fourteen years old selling her body to grow men she doesn't even know

How she wanted to stop having sex each and everyday

But she knew she couldn't because she wouldn't have a place to stay

So this is what she do every single day

HE'S IN THE GANG

He's in the gang he still remains

He hanging near the corner with his friends

Selling what's in his pockets

Until it's nothing left but dead presidents

Everything is like a game

He doesn't care for the love he never had

He the type who doesn't care if he lives or die

He doesn't have nothing to live for in life

Every female he meets he mistreat

Rather your good or bad the same rules apply

If you are his old head or right-hand man

He looks out more than well

Telling him to check someone off the bucket list

He'll do it without even thinking twice it's liking rolling dice

He doesn't fear anything for he been through too much that he could careless

He's sixteen young and reckless cold hearted

He used to come to school

But after seven months he stops showing up

DON'T TELL

Don't tell nobody what I been doing to you

What goes on behind these closed doors

Stay between me and you do you understand me

Be shhhh and quiet and no more harm will come to you

Hide your abuses when go to school

If the teachers ask questions just make up some excuse

Don't ever tell them the truth

Go head try to tell your mom

She won't believe you

You know she loves her men more then she does you

She'll put you right in front of her

Just to save her men from walking out that door

Be shhhh and quiet when I come into your room

Be shhhh and quiet when I'm touching you

Be shhhh and quiet until I'm no longer there

LIFE KEEP PASSING BY

Life keep passing me by

No matter how much I try

You want to pause and rewind

When your young you don't think about life

Until it's too late to think

Always living for today never for tomorrow

When your grade drop

It doesn't matter to you

Since you think you aren't going to live to see the day

You graduating from high school anyway

You use to say how you wanted to go to college

So you could be a basketball player

Now it's just about getting by

You don't even try to make it through

Don't care about life like you used too

It's November now

You don't come to school no more

If you were still here sitting beside me

I would had kept pushing you on

But your dead and now your gone

SHE SCARED

Looking into her eyes there's fear she scared

I want to hold her

Tell her it's okay

That there is a better way

But she looking down at that bridge ready to jump over

I see her I see her clear as day

I'm running towards her yelling please wait

But I can hear her thoughts

What is there to live for

I just lost my only friend

Who was my only sister

Who is now dead and gone

No one to turn to no one to care for the little girl

Who only had a little sister to live for

I see her tears falling from her eyes

The hurt the pain is marked deep under her soul

I yelled again she turns looking my way

I can't quite see her face

But she's a young beautiful girl with long brown hair blowing into the wind

I watch her climb onto the pole of the gate till she was standing on top of it

By that time, I'm just three seconds away from her

She looks my way again saying death can take me too right before she hop's over

I reach for her and caught her hand

When she looked up, I realize it was me

YOUNG KINGS

We were young kings remember just playing around

Trying to figure out different ways to escape from this hell

We had our own little plans on how we were going to make it out

When the time came how we was going to help out

At the end of the day all we had was each other

We didn't have a family until we became brothers

I'm thinking about how you actually understood me

Who actually took the time to actually get to know me

We had the same struggles

The same problems

The same stories

I swear nobody knew how I was feeling

When I find out you got shot and kill

They say you got into an argument and things went left field

I couldn't never see you saying anything too crazy

To the point where you're no longer living anymore

In the end of the day we were just kids

Only seventeen and sixteen just trying to live

Ever snice you past away

I been more ambitious

I drop out of high school just to get my GED

I went straight to college

I'm still going to make the dreams we plan come true

I always remember us saying one of us had too

So, I'm still going to do it just for you

The only difference is it's me instead of you

STRUGGLE

What's living in the struggle

Is when you checking the refrigerator when it's nothing to eat

Sharing the same bed with five different people

Don't got much to live for but you still dreaming

Fighting so much it's like you at war

Hustling just to have a come up

When it never matches up

Someone is always knocking you

Someone is always trying to take the last thing you got

So you have no choice but to be a fighter

You got to be a survivor

You got to take care of yours

Nobody who haven't live this doesn't understand this

This life isn't easy

We carry our struggles on our backs

Some how we still smile

We still glow we still shine

When we make it to the top

Know it wasn't easy

It's a lot of scars you don't see so don't misjudge

Remember you're standing on the other side of the grass

So don't forget this

Some things you really don't know

So be very careful when it comes to judging

Don't be the fool and just assume

CRAZY LIFE

She trying to walk in grow woman shoes

When the shoes barely fit

Trying her best to be older than what she really is

Messing with grow men thinking that's mature

Hanging with the wrong type of friends

Got her miss behaving in school

Mother isn't there

Father was never around

Baby girl is on her own basically raising herself

This is the life she was giving

There's no changing it

She's like fuck the world that's exactly how it is

Hit up a club one night with a couple of her friends

She wasn't even old enough to be there yet she still got in

She seen a man that caught her eyes

That was looking at her all night long

He finally walks up to her

He starting to talk his game to her

Got her smiling got her giggling

Got her a few drinks now she ready to leave with him

She said goodbye to her friends that she'll contact them later

Hop in his car because that wasn't her first time

Took her to a hotel because he had a wife and kids at home

Next day he woke up she was already gone

While getting wash and dress

He finds something she left

It was a beautiful locket that was written mother and daughter

He didn't think nothing of it even when he opened it

But if he actually looks at the picture

He would had realized that was his under-age daughter

CHAPTER 2

Love Gain & Love Lost

SO MANY TIMES

So many times, I try

Some many times, I fell

So many times, I wonder about you and I

So many things we did

So many things that we said

So many things that I didn't tell

If only I had another chance

I would turn everything all around

So many times I seen you

So many times I said hi

I should had walk away and said bye

So many times, I ask myself

Did I make a mistake

Between you and I

In this life we would never know

For you're with someone else and so am I

I just used to wonder about you and I

HE GIVES

He gives me the strength to go on about my day

He holds me when I'm feeling lost or confuse

He kisses me when my soul is singing the sad blues

He makes love to me when I need that special refill to rejoice me

Oh, when he smiles

Oh, my gosh when he smiles

My heart would just stop only for that short movement

He gives me the kind of tenderness that I never even knew existed in a world like this

So, when he questions why I like him

Why I want him

Why he matters to me

I'll simply read him this

He keeps me safe in his heart safely tuck away

Where's nobody able to touch me only him

The best part is he's all mine and I'm all his

I'm just glad I finally found him or should I say him finally finding me

But either way he's more than I need

He's more than I image him to be

This is my king rather he knows he is one or not

I'll make him feel like one to me

The things he got me feeling

It's not like it just sexually or just plan lust

No, it's deeper than anything that lust or sex can instore

He got me feeling like a little girl with a crush

I just love the feeling he gives

I love the way he got me

And I just can't deny it

Snice it's writing all over me

It's like he already blueprinted on me just by the love he gives me alone

That's why you'll see me with this smile or glow on me

Yeah, he's the one who put it one me and I couldn't thank him enough for it

DON'T TAKE

Tell me how many pieces you need from me

Tell me how much I got to give to make you whole

I know I'm not the one who broke you

But you putting me through hell

I'm really trying to figure out what you want

Tell me what's going on with you honestly

Tell me what you feeling the most

Tell me if it's someone new who got you

I know it's not just me

I know I can't be getting lead on

I know everything you said

I know what lays between your mind

When I walk by feeling the coldness

When we make eye contact and get wordless

When you feel something but can't express it

It's more confusing than religion

What's going on we can't even tell no more

We can't connect

We can't react

I rather leave everything in the past

I rather forget about the love we once had

I rather let go before I have a break down

This is no good

This is unhealthy

This is bad for sure

I'll wipe your tears away

Before I'll kiss you goodbye

I'll huge you one more last time

I hope the next stage in life is more beneficial

I hope it's nothing but progress

NOT HERSELF

She doesn't trust the same no more

Everything is different her emotions is not there

She gives herself away

She gives her smiles away

She tries to make other people day

She tries to hide her own pain

Every guy wonders about her

Every guy gets interested when she walks by

Close off she really is

Distance is her middle name

She could make you laugh

She make you forget about your sorrow

She brings joy

That energy she gives

That positive vibe everyone wants a piece of

Love it when she's around

Love it when she speaks her mind

Love it when she got the answer to the problem

Love it when she's can solve them

No one is there for her

No one actually knows her

What they see is what they believe

She going through her own personal battles

That she'll never bring to the table

Only God really knows her name

Only God knows her heart and soul

TELL ME

Tell me if this is love or lust

Tell me if you know the difference between the two

I want to know if your playing around

I'm trying to figure out what's going down

I want to know what I'm really getting myself into

You say you want me but is it true

You say I got you like no one else do

When I come around boy

I can tell the difference boy

I know the feeling I'm getting

No matter what you are saying

Your body language is speaking a whole different language

Tell me if I'm wrong or right

Tell me if I'm not getting straight to the point

I don't want to keep going back and forth

I don't want to keep questing this like we at war

There's no need to raise your voice

There's no need to try to over talk me

When you keep your head down low

I can see the truth inside of you

I can tell your just using it as a sad love song instrumental

When you say you don't know who to trust

It's not like I was every in a rush

I took my time never once did I put up a fuss

I just don't plan on being no fool

If you wanted me you would had show me

If you care for me you would had been there for me

If it wasn't just me, I should had been the only one

You were holding in your arms

Tell me what was the point in seeing me

Tell me what was the point in talking to me

If I couldn't do nothing for you and you couldn't see yourself with me

I just want to know

I just want to know why

I know that's a question you'll never answer

I know that's the reason why I stop caring

That's the reason why you never really did quite get me

WHEN I FIND HIM

I been watching you for a awhile

They say that I'm hopeless for love

That I just can't keep my head out the clouds

That I still be wishing on the stars

Hoping for someone that's really mines

That I might find him some day

We could prove everyone wrong

How love still exists and it still remains strong

But I haven't found you yet

So, I just set and think how we would be

How I would be there for you

How I wouldn't ever compared you to any another man I had

You'll be the only one for me and I'll be the only one for you

You can just talk to me telling me what's on your mind

I'll be the one you vent too

I'll be the one to ask you how was your day

And when you really having bad days

And we can't seem to meet eye to eye

I remember to try my best letting you know this is nothing but a test

That every couple goes through a rough patch but I still won't leave you

Even if we don't meet eye to eye

My heart is forever yours so there are no goodbyes

BAD HABITS

I'm trying to figure out what I'm doing wrong

I'm wondering why you don't pick up no more

Is it something that I said most of those things I never met

All I think about is you and how these other guys can't replace you

But we not doing the same things that we used too

You had me falling for you

You had me missing you when you weren't around

I'm trying figure out if you're playing now

Should I do the same thing

Should I say I'm single now

When all I really want is you

I'm trying to see if you'll come through

None of these females can be me

So, don't start screeching what you had in me with someone new

Let me know what you want me to do

I don't got time for guessing games

I'm just want to know if I'm wasting my time with you

I'm not feeling the distance between us

The communication is falling off

Let me know if you're playing house with another

Let me know if this was all just a front

I know I'm kind of being all blunt

I just really want to know

I know I should take signs instead of words

But I need to hear it just for me to feel it

I'm looking at my phone thinking about calling you

Even if you don't answer I'm still going to say fuck you

Then you'll contact me saying why I'm acting like that

You'll say I need to chill there's no need to trip relax

Then you'll talk game like you always do

Than everything repeats itself like it always do

I LOVED YOU

Yeah, I said it I love you

I'm not going to front on you

I know I didn't say it as often

To you as I was supposed to

I figure I didn't have to

If I show you more than I had too

I put years in with you

Tell me who was really messing with you the way I do

When you lost your right

Who was there holding you

Who was there consoling you

Was it not I was it not me

Saying don't worry I got you

While wiping your tears away from your eyes

Wasn't I even there for you

Even more on those days you had nothing to offer me

No matter what type of struggle you were in

I made sure I never left you

Instead I chosen to help you

I chose to make things alright again

Everybody said you never did deserve me

If they ask me back than

I would say they all wrong about you

Because there wasn't nothing better than you

Only God came before you

Everything I had I made sure you had it too

You were my man

how could you ever dare say I wasn't there for you

Did I not spoil you was I not making love to you

I did my best to try to uplift you try to inspire you

But yet you chose to leave me because I wasn't enough for you

You told me you wanted more of what I was giving only with someone new

I guess you didn't know half of these fucking females can only do half of what I do

Shit I was in love with you

I did more than admire you

I did more than appreciate you

How could you dare say I didn't love you

You must get me confused with those hoes you were fucking around with

If you knew all the things, I gave up for you maybe you would be acting different

but none of that matters to you

I stayed trying to crown you

I stayed trying to make you my king

But you can't crown no man who wasn't born to be no king

I had to find that out the hard way

No matter what I say I still can't put nothing against you

My friends say I'm soft since I chose to forgive you

But I couldn't hate you

Why put more time and energy in

Then I actually did love you

You got a new girl now

I heard she having a son by you

It's crazy how this all happened

After you broke it off with me

If it turns out to be yours

I'm going to take the time out to say congratulations to you

I know I probably shouldn't be saying anything at all to you

I should say fuck you

But I care for you

But I wish the best for you

I hope you truly happy now

I hope she's really the one for you

Now let me focus now

Now let me let this go now

Now let me get right back to making this money cash flow

DO YOU GET ME

I love the sound of his voice

I love the base of it when he talks

He got me smiling

He doesn't even know the reason why

He got my head up in the clouds

God, I got to come back down to earth

Before I get lost in his eyes

I promise this won't happen every time

He won't stay away he love my vibe

I feel like he been waiting it all the time

Distance doesn't last long

Before he starts hitting up my line

He good with his words just like I'm good with mine

We getting caught up

We getting rush up

To the point it scared the hell out of us

We not really trying to get emotional involved

No, we not we got trust issues it's more complicated than we thought

Second guessing goes past our minds

When we together it's a whole different level

That's why stay talking all the time

When was the last time you connected with a person intellectually

It's not even about sex it's more mentally

Want to know how you think

Want to see what you see

It's a difference believe me

Some who wants to help build you up in all means

How many of ya'll really know what I mean

BRAND NEW

How long does it take

For someone start acting different

Is less than a month or a year

Can it be done that same day

Forgetting that you ever care

That nothing was ever real

Number block you go straight to voicemail

Can't use social media you cut off there

Feelings got involved but you don't care

Call someone else up you know they going to be there

Until that other person wants you back

But you curved on them for playing with you like that

Now they in their feeling because they always thought they can get you back

But now they going to call someone else up

Given the same line they just gave you

It doesn't matter as long as it not you that they coming too

You said the hell with them you been doing you and nothing better than focusing on you

PAST HISTORY

I see your full of trouble

While your eyes are lock on me

You say I'm your type

That I got more than what you like

Keeping my distance is what I do best

Avoiding complete conversation

Only saying hi and bye

You're the trouble type and I'm just trying to do myself right

I know it all seems so sweet and beautiful

I know the attraction is the death round

I step more than three steps back

I know your no good

Always hurting everyone you love

Always trying to be controlling

So please excuse me for being in the wrong place at the wrong time

Just pretend to be blind

Just pretend you never seen me

Just pretend our eyes never made eye contact

That I never walk by and you never said hi

That you never ask to know my name

Trouble guys don't mix well when you're trying to do right

I'm not feeling the vibe

I'm not feeling the opposite attraction

I'll kiss it long goodbye into the night

This is nothing but past history

I know one day you'll change

I know one day you'll be a completely different guy

You'll have a whole different mindset

But right now, that's neither the day or the time

FROM THE DISTANCE

I said l love from a distance

I know you messing with the same check

That's why I'm not going back to you

You keep saying you're different

You're not the old you that I once knew

But I don't trust you to believe it

I been a fool for you more than twice

Yeah, I was dumb stupid too

But everybody kept saying love comes with a sacrifice

I know probably won't believe it

But I don't have any more chances to give to you

So, I'll be moving on now

I'm saying goodbye now to everything we once knew

Being in love with you wasn't the best thing to do

I doubted every moment when you were out caught messing around

I just kept saying it wasn't true

There's no hiding it or denying it no more

I won't allow myself to feel sad over it

The love you had for me wasn't the same as mines

If it was you would have never did what you done

Without it being able to hurt you like it's hurting me right now

Those tears you cry you can just wipe away from me

All your secrets all your lies finally came to my eyes

You were living a double life

I guess that's why question was I cheating most of the time

I should have paid attention to the signs

But I was completely happy thought you were too

I thought I was the only women for you

Why ask to get married if I wasn't the one for you

Love is completely blind for sure and that's the God honest truth

I mean shit who knew

I'M PAST THE POINT

See girls might not get it

But I'm pass he fine as hell stage

Yeah you might have waves inside your waves

Your natural curls may out curl goldilocks any day

That gorgeous smile you got that brings out your eyes every time

A body that doesn't need to be redefined

It's more perfect than wine

I can see what you got every time you put some sweatpants on

When it comes to physical attraction you know how to turn it on

But let's step back after I see you got that

Now I want to know does your mental match

What you have to offer that I can actually invest

If all you got is look than you going have to take that left

I'm going to need your intellectual to match

Looks may get you through the door with others

But it only gets you halfway through the door with me

If you don't have no real quality than you just not the one for me

I'm past that stage where looks is not enough for me

Since I am an investor, I have to see what type of stocks you have for me

I'll show you things I have to offer you

It can be a take it or leave it or see where it goes kind of thing

But long story short I hope you got more than looks for me

DO YOU

He said I'm the type of woman he likes

But am I the type you'll value

I don't like mind games

Can you be true because my style is nice

How I carry myself got you wanted to take a bite

But before you get hype just know my standards can be high

I might over work you just to show you

that you can reach the things you thought you couldn't do

You will get a chance if you can prove you are a good man

I can be your ride or die just know everything takes time

So, come to me allow me to explore your mind

I want see to how well you can represent yourself

No this is not a test

It's more like a pop quiz

I want you to make it to the finish line

Come on catch up to these green lights

Tell me which way you flowing so we can float together

I'm all about building and leveling up

so, give me that drive and I'll feed you mines

Let's kiss these hardship goodbye

Let me close your eyes

Let me give you a surprise

Let me show you how well our world can intertwine

It's looks so fine just like old wine

YOUR CHOICE

Tell me if I'm what you're missing

Tell me if I'm what you've been looking for

Since a young little boy

Tell me if I'm the woman you had been dreaming of

You stay confusing me on what you actually want

You want to hold me

You want me near you

You say you miss me

Then you'll push me away

Then you'll stop communicating with me

Then you'll say you can't do this no more

Tell me which one it is

Tell me which mood are you feeling today

Do you want to be all up underneath me

Do you want to be kissing all over me

Saying you want a family

Saying you want a spiritual connection

Saying you want a long-term relationship

Saying you want marriage

Don't you know that takes time

Don't you know that takes efforts

Don't you know that comes with understanding

Not someone who ready to walk out when things don't go as plan

If you don't got the patience your nowhere ready for a long term

Sorry if I had to pop your bubble

Just to let some light in for this situation

But I couldn't allow you to walk away

Without you seeing the full details in this picture

HE GOT YOU

He got you pretty well

He got you feeling yourself

He got you up against that wall

Your body is not your own

Every time he touches you

Every time he kisses you

You give your mind and soul

He knows you pretty well

He knows your different favorite spots

Where every time you say no

When every time you say you can't

He just makes you say yes

He just makes you say you can and will

Every time you open your legs it's a gateway

There's no denying him

There's no leaving him

He got you pretty damn well

He got you feeling things that you didn't know

there's no running away from him now

You say he can be that one

You say can it be this real

He told you what he wanted

He told you he could get it from you

If he ever really put his mind to it

He said he was great with words

He said he knew how to get inside of your heart and mind

You dare him to take that step

You dare him to cross that line

So, he did without even hesitating

He played it every smart

He laid all his cards down just right to get you where you are now

The only damage is you falling in love

You can't seem to let him go

You always want more arounds

You always want more than what he's willing to give

He would say you knew what it was

He would say you knew exactly what I was more willing to offer

I chose you just like you pick me

Don't go asking for more

That's not what we sign up for

I didn't make the rules you did

I told you before don't get upset when things don't go how you plan

I was never the love man

You knew that before I ever approach you

You just thought it would be me and not you

And yeah, I hear about you too

I know things that you do

I just wasn't going to get played no not by you

DOUBLE STANDERS

The double standards belief

She slept with you the first day

Decided to open up her garden to you Unbeknownst to you

The time she took debating rather this was the right thing to do

Even if this was her first time or not

The fact she felt able to trust you

Without being misjudged or misused

You made her feel as though everything was okay

So, when the time came you got what you wanted

Did a lot to convince her you weren't a thief in the night only looking for what he can get and steal

Now you were on a different page we can talk we can chill I'm not really looking for that kind of thing

So, when she opened up her garden, she decided to feed you her fruits

She put all her hard work into growing these things.

For you to mislead her

For you to call her out of her name

I'll advise you to think twice

Before you say another thing

LOVE

I never been in love

So, tell me what it was

I just met you only a few days ago

You already running through my mind

I know I never been in love

But is it possible this could be the first time

When I catch your eyes

It's like a natural high

Caution should be aware

Your unoriginal charm got me floating

Your intelligence got me wondering

Hey handsome tell me where you came from

Did you came from my left or right

I never saw you actually coming

You got me in a daze

While your smile keeps taking me away

I never been in love

I never been in love

Until the day I met you

MY WORTH

Baby I want to know if I'm worth the time of day

Am I worth the love and attention that you might be giving away

I want to know if I'm worth more than diamonds and pearls

Am I worth the wait or patience

Am I worth that extra mile to you

I want to know am I worth the moon and stars that's giving at night

I want to know am I worth the loyalty and respect

Am I worthy to show to your family

Am I worth any other women that you might have your eyes set on

I want to know what I stand as to you as young women

Do I come as something less or something more to you

I want to know am I someone special to you or just a piece of crap to you

I want to know am I worth telling your secrets too

Am I worth being real to

Am I worth holding on to

I want to know am I the one that make you smile

When your world doesn't shine for you

That calms you when you're having a rough time or maybe

Am I just someone you're just playing around with for fun

Am I just someone you're just fronting for

Only to pretend you have an interest for

I want to know am I worth to be cherish by you

I want to know am I worth the effort to make it last with you

Or is possible that I could only be just sex to you

Someone you want when you need her

But when she needs you

You'll walk straight out on her

Than act like y'all never had real conversations before

I want to know what is it between me and you

What's my worth to you

What's my worth to you

I want to know does it mean anything to you

What am I worth to you because if you can't find it or see it

I don't mind showing you

But if you choose not to pay attention to it

   Don't get upset if it happens to walk right pass you

I just wanted to know was I ever worth anything to you

MY JOY

I'm his heart

I'm a part of his soul

I'm one of the reasons why he glows

I give him my love to keep him going

I'm one of his inspirations

I'm his number one supporter along with our daughter

I stand as his reflection

The way I carry myself

The way I speak

The way I hold my head up

It's because of him

Gave me more than confidence

Gave me more than Knowledge

Gave me more than strength

I know not everyone going to understand it

For my man for my loving husband

There's really nothing I can't do

What us together that's living proof

RELATIONSHIP NOT LASTING

I'm trying to figure out why relationship doesn't last forever

Why it's not common no more

You just couldn't solve the problem

Did someone kept lying

Someone being miss treated

Someone out there cheating

Or did the love just fade away

Forgot how to enjoy one another

Forgot how to communicate

Or did someone need space

Or did someone jump in to fast

Rush the whole relationship thing

Or did someone get bored

Someone wanted more

Did someone become insecure

Did someone become unsure

Did ya'll start arguing more

Someone trying to control everything

Started playing games

I'm trying to figure out why it doesn't last no more

Tell me what is forever anymore

DON'T STOP BELIEVING

I know I have my weak movements

Temptation is a bitch

I wish I never did what I did

I wish I never made you cry

I never meant to hurt you

So I apologize rather you accept it or not

I know I was wrong

I know I should had stayed with you

Loving you was never easy

But I keep pushing anyways

I know you probably hate me

You probably turn into something I never wanted you to be

Saying fuck love

It's all about getting money now

When we both know you want more

You airing everything out

I see you're still venting

Got you talking bad about women

Don't get closed off

Don't stop believing because of me

It's good woman out there

Who would do more than me

Who would be better for you than me

I'm sorry that I broke your heart

Your love I couldn't handle

I got scared so I folded

Had you standing by yourself

So please forgive me because you deserve the best

Even if that woman wasn't me

HOW HARD

How hard can you fight for us

How much can you try for us

Can you take your time

Can you listen

Can you actually love everything about us

Even with the good and bad

Can we heal from the past

Can we grow like we tended

I know you love me

You know I love you

So, what are we doing

What's the next move

I'm getting tired of the drama

I want to make love and make up

How can you leave

How can you say goodbye to me

I keep giving you all my energy

I want to rebuild to make us stronger

It's me and you only me and you

I just want to be happy with you

Tell me what's wrong

Tell me what should we work on

Because you're my best friend my best team mate

Your more than a soul mate

I'm not giving you a false dream

I'm giving you reality

So, keep your eyes open

Can you see the beauty in us

Can you see the unconventional love

Can you see the miscommunication that happens sometimes

How people can hate what we have

Try to ruin what we got

We can't listen to the hearsay when it's never proven

Don't compare us to other people relationships

Don't misjudge us

That's how we fall off

That's how the war begins

Now we out talking each other

No one is listening

Let's put out the flames

I don't like how the fires grows

Let's calm down

Let's relax let's rethink

Now tell me what's wrong

Can you take your time

Can we both listening and comprehend what we are saying

Can we see both sides of the story

Don't quite and move on when things get to hard

I just want to grow and move on

GENUINE

Tell me if I'm everything you need in a woman

Tell me if I'm everything you wanted and more

Tell me if you believe I'm the only one that's right for you

That God created me hand made just for you

That I'm where your heart belongs

That I'm more than your home

When you missing me, you'll do anything just to see me

Call me just to hear me say your name

Talking to you night and day when your far away

When we see each other again it's nothing but hugs and kisses

Asking what should we do today

Have a movie night

Have a game night

Or just stay home cuddling and play fighting

It's no need for me to be with someone else besides you

I know for sure your more than my joy

The connection we got is better than two best friends

We can argue we can disagree and still find have peace in each other

When another beautiful woman got her eyes on you

I don't stress it at all when your eyes always lock on me

When I'm gone you constantly looking for me

When you gone, I'm constantly asking for you

Even when we never that far from each other

I don't know why we feel this way

I don't know why we act this way

You give me everything I always need

You make sure I'm on top of my game

You make sure I never give up on my dreams

You even help me bring some of them to reality

Our love is beyond strong all the things we been through as a couple and we still stand strong

I know sometimes we both can be complicated

Not wanting to talk on what's really wrong

Since we learn how to work with each problem

we got better at solving them

We're perfectly imperfect together

Even if we don't match, we still work

There's no need to complain when we're both genuinely happy

CHAPTER 3

Trap

ALONE

I feel alone nobody is trying to move along

They just sit there and just do as they told even though they question it

They won't ever raise up angst it I see it for what is it

Fear in our souls that they blue printed there for control

Can we break this chain can we be set free or would we stay blind

Since we're to scared to face the harsh reality of this time

We all try it at least once some of us make it and some of us don't

If we continue to take this same route there won't be no hope

Our history would be covered in lies with blood laid upon it

Think, think, think for yourselves think for your family or

Friends what's best for them for this whole country because

If we don't the next thing you know we all end up on the same floor

The rich the middle class and the poor at the bottom

Where nobody shines just darkness only in the spot lime

I want to change this world but I can't do it alone

I need my great speakers I need my great leaders we can't be quite no more

This is now war for our gradation least take control

Starting today were saying no more

KEEP YOUR HEAD UP

I want to know how you been

I want to know what's been on your mind

What you got being so distance and towards yourself

What you going through that you feel as
though you can't let me know

Don't you know I can see your pain no matter how hard you try to hide it from me.

Don't you know I'm here if you need me

Don't you know I can wipe away your tears

Even when I'm not there

My words are still able to heal

That I do have a good listening ear

That I can make you laugh out loud even when your soul is crying

I can solve some of your problems

I can make you see things differently to show you that your never really standing alone

That your quietness speaks louder than words

That you can do way more than what you think you can

That your worth way more than what you think you are

I'm not trying to gasp you up I just what to get you thinking more

Maybe no one ever push you that far

Maybe no one never really challenge you in that way before

To let you see the best thing you can do is be competitive between yourself

To really see the different on how much you actually grew from the things you went through

Cause no one understand your pain or reasons why better than you and God

And nothing wrong with getting help sometimes because once in a while we all need

Don't let your pride get in your way from what you're thinking

Don't let it get in the way from asking what you truly want to say

Sometimes people come into your life just to help you keep your up head

And sometimes they don't sometime they want to make you miserable as they are

But for the ones that really do right by you just hold closet because those are the ones that's hard to come by

I know you probably heard this all before

And what I'm speaking is nothing new

Don't go getting anger when people walk in and out your life

Just take what you can learn from it and move on from it

Even if it might come hard at movements

Cause everything can be a lesson and a blessing at the same time

If I was able to show you a different world that's way better than this

I wouldn't mind taking you to it myself

but I'm still trying to figure out where's that place at for myself

If we ever happen to fall off or not talk anymore

I hope this be one of my poems that you'll always remember me by the most

NONE THE LESS

I was told not to cry

When I'm going through hard times

I was told to push through while smiling

Turn a dove into a bean

Flipping money isn't easy

I grind for mines nonstop

If you want it

Best believe you'll bleed for it

I don't take losses

I just reelevate

My parents taught me well

I know when to hold back now

I know when to let lose

I know how to check anyone without their feelings being abused

You don't got to fear me

But I won't ever allow you to disrespect me

How I move most people can't keep up with me

That's why I tell people do your own thing

Everything isn't for everybody and that's the reality

I'm learning while I'm going through my own testimonies

So, if I act up

If I show off

It's because I'm actually finally feeling it now

I know life isn't easy

It's a difference when you had nothing

But somehow still made a way to bring a meal to the table

That's another level of achievement

So, I know how to hustle

So, I don't live in sorrows

Not everyone can feel this

Not everyone can relate to this

But if you are a hustler, you'll understand this

THE GAME

I'm fighting a war that's already been won

I'm giving and trying but I'm already in

I'm counting down the past

I'm counting down how old I am

I can't control anything I'm just reliving everything

I see the same people all over again

We question how many times we met like this

I know it's something that I just can't explain

But once I remember I'll be replaced again

It's a game I'm a part of that I can't win in

The rules are always changing

The game gets harder each time I think I know what's going on

Everything shakes than it breaks than rebuild itself in different forms again

I know I'm a threat the game itself has a target mark on me

Only a few will ever see this

I WANT OUT

If I told all my problems

Do you think you can solve them

I got issues with a lot of pain

I'm trying to be positive

I'm trying to be Inspirational

When I'm living in the gutter

No one actually cares what's goes on around here

People life get taken away at a young age around here

When you go missing

No one is there looking for you

It's too many of us

so, who care if a few of us disappear out of thin air

I'm from the bottom of the bottom

Believe me there is no worst

I don't know how deeper can I go

I don't want to talk about my struggles

I just want a way out

That's the only reason why I came here

I been told you was the one to help

Honestly, I never believe in you

I never thought you was real

I never seen you

Until that day I hear you said my name

I know you are the father of all fathers

You're my God

I never knew how lost I really was until you call me

I been waiting for so long

It's about time I can finally see the sign

LIFE

Letting go is something we all learn

Growing up is a choice that we can't choose

Having nothing or having something it's up to else

We can give or we can take

We can rule the whole world or we can let life be

Rather we're here or not it will always remain

The earth isn't going no where

Meanwhile we're dying every day

It's a cycle that the living has

It's a lot of things that man will never understand

Until we are actually passed on and gone away

Right now, it's nothing but confusion

Nothing but lies nothing but wars going on

The peace the freedom the joy

We think we know what that is

Until you actually feel that spiritually

Than you see its different levels to each one

Freedom there's nothing weighting on you

Peace there's no worries no fears

Joy there's no depression no sadness here

You know what it means to be living without death being able to touch you

But yet we can't completely describe this in a sensible way

TELL WHY PAIN LIVING

Tell me why your standing alone

Tell me why your pushing everyone away

Tell me why your crying

Tell me what's wrong

Tell me what's really on your mind

Why you don't smile no more

Why you don't date no more

Why you don't love no more

Why you don't try no more

Why is something I need to know

Pain comes and goes don't you know

Pain isn't a forever thing

Pain can lead to a lot of things if you keep holding on

Pain shouldn't be the last thing that remains

Living on is something you should do

Living for you might bring a change

Living for now not the day before

Living for something new because the old is old news

I SEE A DIFFERENT

It's a war going on

How many of us can tell

We fighting over different areas of the city

Some parts we can't cross

Some parts are getting buy out for a higher cost

I see separation you can tell the difference between an upcoming neighborhood

When people with more wealth start coming in

They make the schools better

That was once an improperly community

After a while you'll see the people who originally lived there moving out

Only because they can't afford their own house anymore

Since their neighborhood value went up

What I'm speaking in facts

You'll see it happening right around Temple University College

Were they try to buy more people house's

You'll see how the neighborhood change

It's not all bad but it's not all good

It's a lot of Gender vacation going and I don't know how many people understood

ALREADY BORN WITH A DISADVANTAGE

Rather I have a child that's light skin or dark skin

They would still be treated the same

Being look as less than a human bean

No matter the knowledge I may give them

The wisdom I put on them

They could still be look as Ignorant

Even if they're smarter than everyone in the class room

See color makes a different like beauty does for someone who never had it

I see a lot of things and a lot of it I question

Racism and discrimination still exist

Those who chose to be blind to it are those who can't handle the reality for what it is

How black people is label as

Just open your eyes to find out

If you were to watch the news what would you see

Would it be a bunch of negativities on what is going on in a black community

I can see the sign it's not a black on black crime

We're just divided it's been that way since slavery so more than 400 years since it's still happening daily

MY FATHER

See my father told me at a young age

How I was a young Queen

That my beauty might strike some

How my Knowledge and wisdom could Intimidate

That the color of my skin is hated

Without understanding the full reason why

This is what I knew

I saw this most of the time

My father try to teach me how my life would be different

Some people just hate you even when you didn't do nothing wrong

My Father told me at a young age

How I was a young Queen

How I was going have to work harder than some

That I had to be better just to over come

OLD SOUL

Would you believe me

If I told you I been here before

I'm not saying once or twice

I can't remember how many times I die

Or how many times God sent me back to this earth

I 'am an old soul you know

You can tell sometimes

On the wisdom I give beyond my youth

I know a lot of things somethings I just forget

It's like a process that it has

After being reborn some many times

It's like a mark that never goes a way

I'm old soul living in a young age

I been here before

Would you believe me

If I told you my real age

I seen mostly everything just in different ways

History has a habit of repeating itself with me

So therefore, it wouldn't be a risk

If I say I'll see you again someday

In a different century in a different age

I been here before

Tell God don't send me back no more

Tell me can you guess my age

GOD CRY

When it's pouring down raining outside

You can see God eyes full of tears

That's the only time God cries

That people actually get to see

But don't realize it's there

When God is hurt

You can feel the pain

Only when it rains

When the lighting comes

It's like a broken smile

That's high in the sky

When you hear the thunder

You can hear the pain

If you ever listen to the rain

BLACK MEN

I love my black men for many reasons

I could never say their worthless

I could never say they don't make great father fingers

That they're not one of the best leaders

That they're not one of the best educators across the history of man

I love my black men for many reasons

How they just can't be so easily defeated

How they overcome many of their worst trials

Despite their setbacks that are giving

Despite the laws that set up against them

They still tend to strive everyday

They still stand strong in everyway

I love my black men for many reasons plus more

BROKEN QUEENS

If I ever catch a broken Queen

Yeah, I see her soul

My main goal would to be to let her shine by giving mines

By showing her, she is still strong

No matter what people think of her

She's better than rubies and gold

Her wisdom is worth more than her clothes

Since we all have bad days sometimes

I'm here to help on whatever I have to fix

I always have my tools with me

No matter what life throws

You may forget this

You may not even remember me after this

I stay doing a pretty good job on letting what's needed to be known

when comes to fixing broken Queens

whenever your tried

Whenever you can't fight your battle no more

I come in play I set everything in place

I know where everything belongs before you even tell me

Don't worry you can finally rest take your break it's well deserves

Whatever you weren't able to finish

I'll complete it for you

When your back on track more than ready to rule

I'll gladly walk back to my thrown

I HOPE

You can give your all

They still watch you fall

You can give your last

They still won't probably appreciate it

You can show them unconditional love

They still might toss it in the trash

Not everyone is worth your time

Not everyone is worth that helping hand

Can't keep giving every last part of you

Can't do it without losing that same energy you give

Don't get worn out by people out here

Don't get caught up

I hope you really be safe in this world

I SEE

I see the curiosity in your eyes

I see the excitement on your face

I see the potential that stands in you

I see the innocents that life didn't take away

I see the child in you still plays

Your pretty calm like this summer breeze

Your pretty wise for your age

Your beauty grows within time

Your light is something only a select few can see

Some people envy you

Some people really try to destroy you

But it's something on you that shatters you

I see that spiritual shield on you

If you didn't know I'll be the one telling you

Someone really protecting you

I just can't see who

TO THE MAN WHO MADE IT

I told him to never stop grinding even when you're fully successful in it

Always keep hustling so the money never stops coming in

Now he stacking up his paper until his safe can't take it

Watching out for those takers knowing he was one of them

But all that change when he started focusing on himself

Not listening to the negativity

He shining and blinding everybody who try to barry him

To the top he goes

Ask him how he feels

He'll said more than good he's feeling great

Family not starving

No more living in property

Got good credit I'm longer in debt

He's always watching out for people who be trying to get him

Those females who be wanting him to slip up

Making it out was all just a dream

Now since it's his reality there's no going back

To the nightmares he was living

Who said hard work doesn't pays off

Can't tell him about pain

Can't tell him about losses

Best believe he been through it all

He had that desire

He had that fire

So, when he came up it wasn't that surprising

But now everyone wants to be around him

Don't got time for the liars

He only breaking bread with those who he was struggling with

Not everyone is welcome to his new life that he created

Some people going to hate it but it doesn't matter

HOW MAKING IT OUT STARTED

Hood men is what she like

Since her daddy was of them

Always carry his pipe

His was on the counter every other night

Trying to get that money right

Trying to get his family out the ghetto just so his kids can have a better life

No doubt about it he was hustler all the way

But got caught up one day when policemen came and got him

He went down with the charges

All he was thinking about who was going to raise his son

Teach him how to be a man better than he can and it was no one

A pusher man he stops being

Told his baby mom she was going to finish college

Because one of them got to be successful

If it wasn't going to be him

he was going to make sure it was going to be her

Now he's only working to help his baby mom through school

Who eventually became his wife

She graduated on the freshmen year of their oldest daughter going to college

NO NEGATIVITY

Don't let the Negativity hold you down

Keep your head up baby boy

There's always a reason to smile

Things can always be worst

And things can always be harder

I know there's a lot pain that's giving around

But don't you condone it don't you receive it

Everything can work out for different reasons

The depression you're in has its own season

When you have set backs

That doesn't mean it's all over

Nine out of ten you can overcome that

All depending on where your head is at

What I'm trying to give you is motivation

I don't want you to feel hopeless inside

I came here to break that

I came here to unchain you

I came here to open your eyes

I want you to see that you can make it

I want to see you living not just alive

I'M NOT SUPPOSE TOO

Can you see these chains on me

One on my neck two on my feet and hands

I'm not allowed to move

I'm not allowed to grow

I'm supposed to be ignorant

Unwise uneducated

Than I'm supposed to pass this on to my sons and daughters

I'm supposed to have fear instead of Courage

I'm not allowed to be outspoken

I'm supposed to sit here and be quit

I was told I couldn't protect my husband

I was told I couldn't be able to covers his wounds and scars

I was told I wouldn't be able to heal him

That I wouldn't be able to help him

When his cuts are bleeding as deep as mines

I'm not allowed to dream

I'm not allowed to have hope

No, I can't see the bigger picture

I got to be hopeless left in despair

I'm supposed to be look down on not cherish

It's forbidden it's like a sin

Can't Recognize my beauty

Can't recognize my strengths

Can't recognize my intelligence

That's a whole another interaction involving disgrace

I'm unwanted women who can't be love

This train of thought is supposed to outlast me

Even after my death even after my time

That's the only thing that's supposed to grow and carry on

It was programed before me

Before my mother and her mother before her

But I'll be damn if this is me

So, I started changing history

As you can see, I broke those fucking chains off me

SISTER

This is my sister

Even though we are not the same color

She was taught she was better

Since the color of her skin is white and not blackish

White America said it made a difference

But yet this is still my sister

My blood streams run in hers

She was taught to hate me, even though I love her everyday

She was told not to conversate with me

If it was to speak to me it would only be to remind me my place

This is my sister that I cater to

That was taken from me

I help her everyday made her life a lot easier in many ways

My sister who denies me

My sister who forgot me

I'm still apart of you in every way

White America can't white that away

It's in our DNA can trace it back to how you are my sister all over again

But that's another story for another day I still love you anyway

www.ingramcontent.com/pod-product-compliance
Lightning Source LLC
LaVergne TN
LVHW060159080526
838202LV00052B/4171